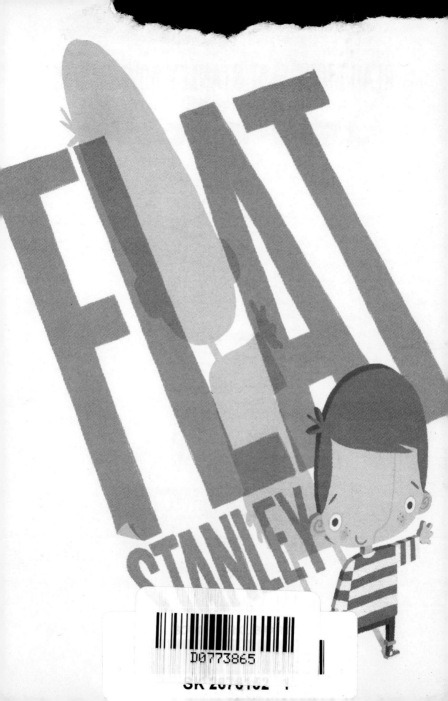

FLAT STANLEY

# READ MORE FLAT STANLEY ADVENTURES
### by
# JEFF BROWN

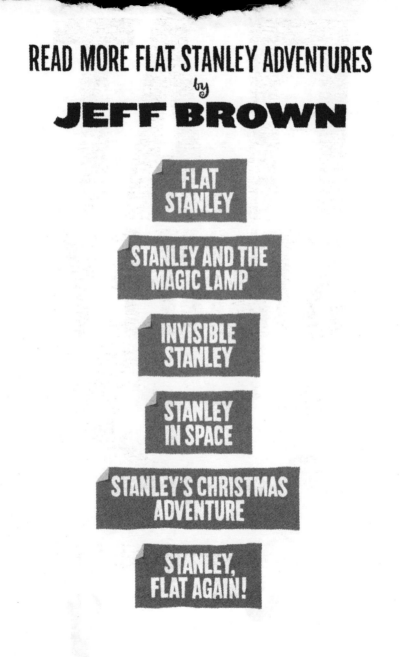

FLAT
STANLEY

STANLEY AND THE
MAGIC LAMP

INVISIBLE
STANLEY

STANLEY
IN SPACE

STANLEY'S CHRISTMAS
ADVENTURE

STANLEY,
FLAT AGAIN!

# FLAT STANLEY

## STANLEY AND THE MAGIC LAMP

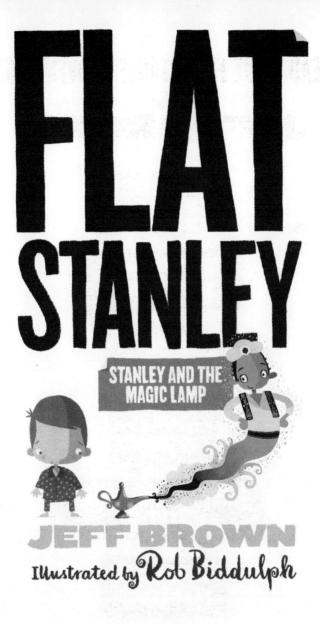

**JEFF BROWN**

Illustrated by Rob Biddulph

EGMONT

For Sidney and Lewis

First published in Great Britain 1985
by Methuen Children's Books Ltd
This edition published 2017
by Egmont UK Limited
The Yellow Building, 1 Nicholas Road, London W11 4AN

Text copyright © 1985 Jeff Brown
Illustrations copyright © 2017 Rob Biddulph

ISBN 978 1 4052 8806 4

www.egmont.co.uk

A CIP catalogue record for this title is available from the British Library

Printed and bound in Great Britain by the CPI Group

67673/1

# CONTENTS

# MEET THE LAMBCHOP FAMILY

**STANLEY**          **ARTHUR**

**MRS LAMBCHOP**     **MR LAMBCHOP**

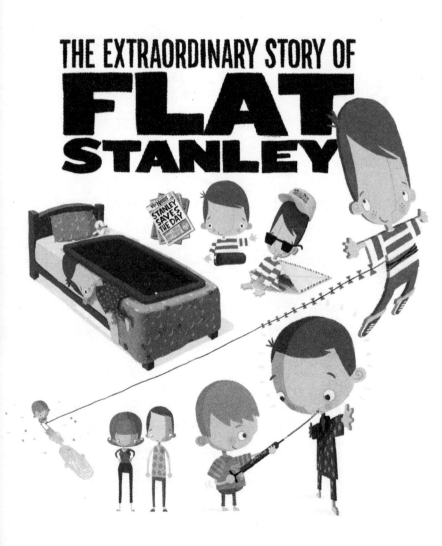

Once there was an ordinary kid called

Stanley Lambchop. A bulletin board

squashed him flat as a pancake.

Flat Stanley became famous − he even

foiled the art robbery of the century!

Stanley's little brother Arthur managed

to reinflate Stanley with a bicycle

pump, but ever since weird stuff just

keeps happening to Stanley . . .

# PROLOGUE

Once upon a very long time ago, way before the beginning of today's sort of people, there was a magical kingdom in which everyone lived forever, and anyone of importance was a genie, mostly the friendly kind. The few wicked genies kept out of sight in mountain caves or at the bottoms of rivers. They had no wish to provoke the great Genie King, who ruled very comfortably from an enormous palace with many towers and courtyards, and gardens with reflecting pools.

The Genie King took a special interest

in the genie princes of the kingdom, and was noted for his patience with their high spirits and desire for adventure.

The Genie Queen, in fact, thought he was *too* patient with them, and she said so one morning in the throne room, where the King was studying reports and proposals for new magic spells.

'Training, that's what they need. Discipline!' She adjusted the Magic Mirror on the throne-room wall. 'Florts and collibots! Granting wishes, which is what they'll be doing one day, is serious work.'

'Florts yourself! You're too hard on these lads,' said the Genie King, and then he frowned. 'This report here, though, says that one of them has been behaving very badly indeed.'

'Haraz, right?' said the Queen. 'He's the worst. What a smarty!'

The Genie King sent a thought to summon Prince Haraz, which is all such a ruler has to do when he wants somebody, and a moment later the young genie flew into the throne room, did a triple flip, and hovered in the air before the throne.

'That's no way to present yourself!' The Queen was furious. 'Really!'

Prince Haraz grinned. 'What's up?'

'You are!' said the King. 'Come down here!'

'No problem,' said the Prince, landing.

'It seems you have been playing a great many magical jokes,' said the King, tapping the reports before him. 'Very *annoying* jokes, such as causing the army's carpets to fly only in circles, which made all my soldiers dizzy.'

'That was a good one!' laughed the Prince.

'And turning the Chief Wizard's wand

into a sausage while he was casting a major spell, you did that?'

'Ha, ha! You should have seen his face!' said the Prince.

'Stop laughing!' cried the Queen. 'Oh, this is shameful! You should be heavily punished!'

'He's just a boy, dear, only two hundred years old,' said the King. 'But I'll –'

'Who knows what *more* he's done?' said the Queen, turning to the Magic Mirror. 'Magic Mirror, what other silly jokes has this fellow played?'

The Magic Mirror squirted apple juice all over her face and the front of her dress.

'Oooooohh!' The Queen whirled around. 'Florts and collibots! I know who's responsible for *that!*'

Prince Haraz blushed and tried to look sorry, but it was too late.

'That does it!' said the Genie King. 'Lamp duty for you, you rascal! One thousand years of service to a lamp.' He turned to the Queen. 'How's that, my dear?'

'Make it two thousand,' said the Queen, drying her face.

# CHAPTER 1
## PRINCE HARAZ

Almost a year had passed since Stanley Lambchop got over being flat, which he had become when his big bulletin board settled on him during the night. It had been a pleasant, restful time for all the Lambchops, as this particular evening was.

Dinner was over. In the living room, Mr Lambchop was reading and Mrs Lambchop was mending socks.

'How nice this is, my dear,' Mr

Lambchop said. 'I am enjoying my newspaper, and your company, and the thought of our boys studying in their room.'

'Let us hope they *are* studying, George,' said Mrs Lambchop. 'So often they find excuses not to work.'

Mr Lambchop chuckled. 'They are very imaginative,' he said. 'No doubt of that.'

In their bedroom, Stanley and his younger brother, Arthur, had in fact begun their homework. They wore pyjamas, and over his Arthur also wore his Mighty Man T-shirt, which helped him to concentrate.

On the desk between them was what they supposed to be a teapot – a round, rather squashed-down pot with a curving spout, and a knob on top for lifting. A wave had rolled it up onto the beach that summer, right to Stanley's feet, and since Mrs Lambchop was very fond of old furniture and silverware, he had saved it as a gift for her birthday, now only a week away.

The pot was painted dark green, but streaks of brownish metal showed through where the green had rubbed off. To see if polishing would make it shine,

Stanley rubbed the knob with his pyjama sleeve.

*Puff!* Black smoke came from the spout.

'Yipes!' Arthur said. 'It's going to explode!'

'Teapots don't explode.' Stanley rubbed again. 'I just –'

*Puff! Puff! Puff!* They came rapidly now, joining to form a small cloud in the air above the desk.

'Look out!' Arthur shouted. 'Double yipes!'

The black cloud swirled within itself, and its blackness became a mixture of brown and blue. A moment more, and it began to lose its cloud shape; arms appeared, and legs, and a head.

'Ready or not, here I come!' said a clear young voice.

And then the cloud was completely gone, and a slender,

cheerful-looking body
hovered in the air
above the desk.
He wore a sort
of decorated
towel on
his head,
a loose
blue shirt,
and curious,
flapping brown
trousers, one
leg of which had
snagged on the
pot's spout.
'Florts!' said the boy,
shaking his leg. 'Collibots!
I got the puffs right, and
the scary cloud, but – there!'

Unsnagged, he floated down to the floor
and bowed to Stanley and Arthur.

'Who rubbed?' he asked

Neither of the brothers could speak.

'Well, *someone* did. Genies don't
just drop in, you know.' The boy bowed
again. 'How do you do? I am Prince Fawzi
Mustafa Aslan Mirza
Melek Namerd Haraz.
Call me Prince Haraz.'

Arthur gasped and
dived under his bed.

'What's the matter with
him?' the genie asked.
'And who are you, and
where am I?'

'I'm Stanley Lambchop,
and this is the United
States of America,'

Stanley said. 'That's my brother Arthur under the bed.'

'Not a very friendly welcome,' said Prince Haraz. 'Especially for someone who's been cooped up in a lamp.' Frowning, he rubbed the back of his neck. 'Florts! One thousand years, with my knees right up against my chin. This is my first time out.'

'I must have gone crazy,' said Arthur from under the bed. 'I am just going to lie here until a doctor comes.'

'Actually, Prince Haraz, you're here sort of by accident,' Stanley said. 'I didn't even know that pot was a lamp. Was it the rubbing? Those puffs of smoke, I mean, that turned into you?'

'Were you scared?' The genie laughed. 'Just a few puffs, I thought, and then I'll *whoooosh* up the spout!'

'Scaring *me* wasn't fair,' said Arthur, staying under the bed. 'I just live in this room because Stanley's my brother. It's his lamp, and he's the one who rubbed it.'

'Then he's the one I grant wishes for,' said Prince Haraz. 'Too bad for you.'

'I don't care,' said Arthur, but he did.

'Can I wish for anything?' Stanley asked. 'Anything at all?'

'Not if it's cruel or evil, or really nasty,' said Prince Haraz. 'I'm a lamp genie, you see, and we're the good kind. Not like those big jar genies. They're stinkers! Take my advice and stay away from big jars and urns – and if you do see one, don't rub it.'

'Wish for something, Stanley,' said Arthur, sounding suspicious. 'Test him out.'

'Wait,' Stanley said. 'I'll be right back.'

He went out into the living room, where Mr and Mrs Lambchop were still sitting quietly enjoying themselves.

'Hey!' he said. 'Guess what?'

'Hay is for horses, Stanley, not people,'

said Mr Lambchop from behind his newspaper. 'Try to remember that.'

'Excuse me,' Stanley said. 'But you'll never guess –'

'My guess is that you and Arthur have not yet finished your homework,' said Mrs Lambchop, looking up from her mending. 'In fact, you can hardly have begun.'

'We *were* going to do it,' said Stanley, talking very fast, 'but I have this pot that turned out to be a lamp, and when I rubbed it smoke came out and then a genie, and he says I can wish for things, only I thought maybe I should ask you first. Arthur got scared, so he's hiding under the bed.'

Mr Lambchop chuckled. 'When your studying is done, my boy,' he said. 'But no treasure chests full of gold and diamonds, please. Think of the taxes we would pay!'

'There is your answer, Stanley,' said Mrs Lambchop. 'Now back to work, please.'

'Okay, then,' said Stanley, going out.

Mrs Lambchop laughed. 'Chests full of gold and diamonds, indeed. Taxes! George, you are very amusing.'

Behind his newspaper, Mr Lambchop smiled again. 'Thank you, my dear,' he said.

# CHAPTER 2
## THE ASKIT BASKET

'I told them, but they didn't believe me,' Stanley said, back in the bedroom.

'Of course they didn't.' Arthur was still under the bed. 'Who'd believe that a whole person could puff out of a pot?'

'It's not a *pot*,' said Prince Haraz. 'And this is a ridiculous way to carry on a conversation. Please come out. I apologise for the puffs.'

Arthur crawled from under the bed. 'No more scary stuff?'

'I promise,' the genie said, and they shook hands.

Arthur could hardly wait now. 'Try it Stanley,' he said. 'Try a wish.'

'We're not allowed,' Stanley said. 'Not till our homework is done.'

'What's homework?' Prince Haraz asked.

The brothers stared at him, amazed, and then Stanley explained. The genie shook his head.

'*After* schooltime, when you could be having fun?' he said. 'Where I come from, we just let Askit Baskets do the work.'

'Well, whatever *they* are, I wish I had one,' said Stanley, forgetting he was not supposed to wish.

Prince Haraz laughed. 'Oh? Look behind you.'

Turning, Stanley and Arthur saw a large straw basket about the size of a beach ball and decorated with green and red zigzag stripes, floating in the air above the desk.

'Yipes!' said Arthur. 'More scary stuff!'

'Don't be silly,' said the genie. 'It's a perfectly ordinary Askit Basket. Whatever you want to know, Stanley, just ask it.'

Feeling rather foolish, Stanley leaned forward and spoke to the basket.

'I, uh . . . that is . . . uh,' he said. 'I'd like, uh . . . can I have answers for my maths homework? It's the problems on page twenty of my book.'

The basket made a steady *huuuummm* sound, and then the hum stopped and a man's voice rose from it, deep and rich like a TV announcer's.

'Thank you for calling Askit Basket,' it said. 'Unfortunately, all our Answer Genies are busy at the present time, but your questions have been received, and you will be served by the first available personnel. While you wait, enjoy a selection by The Geniettes. This message will not be repeated.'

Stanley stared at the Askit Basket. Music was coming out of it now, the sort of soft, faraway music he had heard in the elevators of big office buildings.

Prince Haraz shrugged. 'What can you do? It's a very popular service.'

There was a *click* and the music stopped. Now a female voice, full of bouncy good cheer, came from the basket. 'Hi! This is Shireen. Thanks a whole bunch for waiting, and I would like at this time to give you your answers.

HI! THIS IS SHIREEN.

The first answer is: five pears, six apples, eight bananas. The second answer is: Tom is four years old, Tim is seven, Ted is eleven. The third –'

'Let me get a pencil!' Stanley shouted. 'I can't remember all this!'

'A written record, created especially for your own personal convenience, is in the basket, sir,' said the cheery voice. 'Thanks for calling Askit Basket, and have a nice day!'

'Wait!' Lifting the lid of the basket, Stanley saw a sheet of paper with all his answers on it. 'Oh, good!' he said. 'Thank you. Can my brother talk now, please?'

Arthur cleared his throat. 'Hello Shireen,' he said. 'This is Arthur Lambchop speaking. For English, I'm supposed to write about "What I Want to

Be". Could I have it printed out, please, like Stanley's maths?'

The answer came right away. 'Certainly, Mr Lambchop. Just a teeny-tiny moment now, while we make sure the handwriting – There! All done, Mr Lambchop!'

What I want to Be
by ARTHUR LAMBChoP

When I grow up I want to be
President of the United
States so THAT I can make a law
not to have any moRE waRs.
And get to meet astronaut astronauts.
And I would like to be
HANdsome, only not have to
Go out with girls who WANT to
to get all dressed up. Most
of all I would like to Be
the strongest man in THE
world, like MIGHTy MAN,
not to hurt people,
but so everybody would be
extRA nice to me.
The End.

Arthur opened the basket and found a sheet of lined paper covered with his own handwriting. He read it aloud.

Arthur smiled. 'That's pretty good!' he said. 'Just what I wanted to say, Shireen.'

'I'm so glad,' said the Askit Basket. 'Bye bye now!'

Stanley and Arthur called goodbye, and then Prince Haraz plucked the basket out of the air and set it on the desk beside his lamp.

'There! Homework's done,' he said. 'That was an awfully ordinary sort of wish, Stanley. Isn't there something special you've always wanted? Something exciting?'

Stanley knew right away what he wanted most. He had always loved animals; how exciting it would be to have his own zoo! But that would take up too much space, he thought. Just one animal then, a truly unusual pet. A lion? Yes! What fun it would be to walk down the street with a pet lion on a leash!

'I wish for a lion!' he said. 'Real, but friendly.'

'Real, but friendly,' said the genie. 'No problem.'

Stanley realised suddenly that a lion would scare people, and that an elephant would be even greater fun.

'An elephant, I mean!' he shouted. 'Not a lion. An elephant!'

'What?' said Prince Haraz. 'An eleph–? Oh, collibots! Look what you made me do!'

A most unusual head had formed in the air across the room, a head with an elephant's trunk for a nose, but with small, neat, lion-like ears. A lion's mane appeared behind the head, but then came an elephant's body and legs in a brownish-gold lion colour, and finally a little grey elephant tail with a pretty gold ruff at the tip. All together, these parts made an animal about the size of a medium lion or a small elephant.

'My goodness!' said Stanley. 'What's that?'

'A Liophant.' Prince Haraz sounded annoyed. 'It's your fault, not mine. You overlapped your wish.'

The Liophant opened his mouth wide and went *Grrowll-HONK!* a half roar, half snort that made everyone jump. Then he sat back on his hind legs and went *pant-pant-pant* like a puppy, looking quite nice.

'Well, we got the friendly part right,' said the genie. 'The young ones mostly are.'

Stanley patted him, and Arthur tickled behind the neat little ears. The Liophant licked their hands, and Stanley was not at all sorry that he had mixed up his wish.

Just then, a knock sounded on the bedroom door, and Mrs Lambchop's voice called out, 'Homework done?'

'Come in,' Stanley said, not stopping to think, and the door opened.

'How very quiet you –' Mrs Lambchop began, and then she stopped.

Her eyes moved slowly about the room from Prince Haraz to the Askit Basket, and on to the Liophant.

'Gracious!' she said.

Prince Haraz made a little bow. 'How do you do? You are the mother of these fine lads, I suppose?'

'I am thank you,' said Mrs Lambchop. 'Have we met? I don't seem to –'

'This is Prince Haraz,' Stanley said. 'And that's a Liophant, and that's an Askit Basket.'

'Guess what,' said Arthur. 'Prince Haraz is a genie, and he'll let Stanley have anything he wants.'

'How very generous!' Mrs Lambchop said. 'But I'm not sure . . .' Turning, she called into the living room. 'George, you had better come here! Something quite unexpected has happened.'

'In a moment,' Mr Lambchop called back. 'I am reading an unusual story in my newspaper, about a duck who watches TV.'

'This is even more unusual than that,' she said, and Mr Lambchop came at once.

'Ah, yes,' he said, looking about the room. 'Yes, I see. Would someone care to explain?'

'I tried to before,' Stanley said. 'Remember? About the lamp, and –'

'Wait, dear,' said Mrs Lambchop.

The Liophant was making snuffling, hungry sounds, so she went off to the kitchen and returned with a large bowl full of hamburger mixed with warm milk. While the Liophant ate, Stanley told what had happened.

'Unusual indeed! And what a fine opportunity for you, Stanley,' Mr Lambchop said when he had heard everything, and then he frowned. 'But I do not approve of using the Askit Basket for homework, boys. Nor will your teachers, I'm afraid.'

'My plan is, let's not tell them,' Arthur said.

Mr Lambchop gave him a long look. 'Would you take credit for work you have not done?'

Arthur blushed. 'Oh, no! When you put it that way . . . Gosh, of course not! I wasn't thinking. Because of all the excitement, you know?'

Mr Lambchop wrote NOT IN USE on a piece of cardboard and taped it to the Askit Basket.

'It is too late for any more wishing tonight,' said Mrs Lambchop. 'Prince Haraz, there is a folding bed in the cupboard, so you will be quite comfortable here with Stanley and Arthur. Tomorrow is Saturday, which we Lambchops always spend together in the park. You will join us, I hope?'

'Thank you very much,' said the genie, and he helped Stanley and Arthur set up the bed.

The Liophant was already asleep, and after Mr and Mrs Lambchop had said good night, Mrs Lambchop picked up his bowl. 'Gracious!' she said, putting out the light. 'Three pounds of the best hamburger, and he ate it all!'

It was quite dark in the bedroom, but some moonlight shone through the window. From their beds, Stanley and Arthur could see that Prince Haraz was still sitting up on his. For a moment they all kept silent, listening to the gentle snoring of the Liophant, and then the genie said, 'Sorry about that. It's having all that nose, probably.'

'It's okay,' Arthur said sleepily. 'Do genies snore?'

'We don't even sleep,' said Prince Haraz. 'Your mother was so kind, I didn't want to tell her. It might have made her feel bad.'

'I'll try to stay awake for a while, if you want to talk,' Stanley said.

'No thanks,' the genie said. 'I'll be fine. After all those years alone in the lamp, it's nice just having company.'

# CHAPTER 3
## IN THE PARK

Everyone slept late and enjoyed a large breakfast, particularly the Liophant, who ate two more pounds of hamburger, five bananas, and three loaves of bread.

Then, since all the Lambchops enjoyed playing tennis, they set out with their rackets for the courts in the big park close by. Since his genie clothes would make people stare, Prince Haraz borrowed slacks and a shirt from

Stanley, and came along to watch.

In the street, they met Ralph Jones, an old college friend of Mr Lambchop's, whom they had not seen for quite some time.

'Nice running into you, George, and you too, Mrs Lambchop,' Mr Jones said. 'Hello, Arthur. Hello, Stanley. Aren't you the one who was flat? Rounded out nicely, I see.'

'You always did have a fine memory, Ralph,' Mr Lambchop said. 'Let me introduce our house guest, Prince Haraz. He is a foreign student, here to study our ways.'

'How do you do,' said the genie. 'I am Fawzi Mustafa Aslan Mirza Melek Namerd Haraz.'

'How do you do,' Mr Jones said. 'Well,

I must be on my way. Goodbye, Lambchops.
Nice to have met you, Prince Fawzi
Mustafa Aslan Mirza Melek
Namerd Haraz.'

'He *does* have a wonderful memory,'
Mrs Lambchop said, as Mr Jones walked
away.

They set out for the park again.

'Wouldn't Mr Jones be surprised if he
learned Prince Haraz was a genie?' Mrs
Lambchop said. 'The whole world would
be amazed. Gracious! We'd all be famous,
I'm sure.'

'I was famous once, when I was flat,'
Stanley said. 'I didn't like it after a while.'

'I remember,' said Mrs Lambchop.
'Nevertheless, I would enjoy discovering
for myself what being famous feels like.'

Prince Haraz looked at Stanley, his

eyebrows raised in a questioning way. Stanley gave a little nod, and the genie smiled and nodded back.

Just ahead, near the entrance to the park, was the Famous Museum of Art, one of the most important buildings in the city. A guided-tour bus, filled with visitors from all over the United States and from many foreign countries, had stopped in front of the museum, and the driver was lecturing his passengers through a megaphone.

'Over where those trees are, that's our magnificent City Park!' shouted the driver. 'Here, on the right, is the Famous Museum of Art, with the world's most expensive paintings, statues, and − Oh, what a surprise! We're in luck today, folks! That's Mrs George Lambchop,

coming right toward us! Harriet
Lambchop herself, in person! Right there,
with the tennis racket!'

Cries of astonishment and pleasure
rose from the tourists as they turned in
their seats to stare where the driver was
pointing.

'What's this?' said Mr Lambchop.
'Is that man talking about you, Harriet?'

'I think so,' said Mrs Lambchop. 'Oh, my
goodness! They're coming!'

The tourists were rushing out of the
bus, waving cameras and autograph
pads. A Japanese family reached Mrs
Lambchop first, all with
cameras.

'Please, Lambchop lady,'
said the husband, bowing
politely. 'Honour to take picture, yes?'

'Of course,' said Mrs Lambchop. 'I hope you are enjoying our country. But why *my* picture? I'm not –'

'No, no! Famous, famous! Famous Lambchop lady!' cried the Japanese family, taking pictures as fast as they could.

Mrs Lambchop understood suddenly that her wish had been granted. 'Thank you, Stanley and Prince Haraz!' she said. 'What fun!'

She posed graciously for all the tourists and signed dozens of autographs. This took almost half an hour, and at the entrance to the park she was recognized again, and had to do more posing and signing.

It was by now mid-morning, and all the

park's tennis courts were occupied, but the Lambchops' disappointment vanished quickly when they saw a crowd gathered by one court, and learned that Tom McRude, the world's best tennis player, was about to lecture and demonstrate his strokes. Tom McRude had a terrible temper and very bad manners, but because of his wonderful tennis a great many people had come to see him. The Lambchops and Prince Haraz managed to squeeze close to the court, next to the television news cameras that were covering the event.

'None of you can ever be a great tennis player like me,' Tom McRude was saying, out on the court. 'But at least you can have the thrill of getting to see me.'

A little old lady in the crowd gave a tiny

sneeze, and he glared at her. 'What's the matter with you, Granny?' he shouted.

The old lady burst into tears, and her friends led her away.

'What a mean fellow!' Prince Haraz whispered to Stanley.

'I can't stand old sneezing people!' said Tom McRude. 'Okay, now I'm going to show how I hit my great forehand! First, I –'

'Hold it, Tom!' called the television director. 'We've just spotted Harriet Lambchop in the crowd here. What a break! Maybe we can get her to say a few words to our audience!'

Even Tom McRude was impressed. '*The* Harriet Lambchop? Here? In person?'

'Swing those cameras this way, fellows!' The director ran to where the Lambchops were standing, and held a microphone out to Mrs Lambchop.

'Wonderful to see you!' he said. 'Everybody wants to know what you think.

What about the foreign situation? What's your favourite colour? Go to discos? Do you sleep in pyjamas or a nightdress?'

'Isn't that rather personal?' said Mr Lambchop.

'George, please . . .' Mrs Lambchop smiled at the director. 'Thank you for your kind welcome,' she said into the microphone, 'and I would just like to say at this time that I hope all my fans are having a lovely day here in this delightful park.'

The crowd cheered and waved, and Mrs Lambchop waved back and blew a few kisses. Tom McRude was so jealous of the attention she was getting that he whacked a tennis ball angrily over the trees behind the court. Noticing, Mrs Lambchop spoke again into the microphone.

'And now,' she said, 'do let us hear what this champion athlete has to tell us about tennis.'

'Yeah!' growled Tom McRude at the TV man. 'Get those cameras back on me!'

When the cameras had swung back to him again, he said, 'Now I want a volunteer, so that I can demonstrate how terrible most players are compared to me.'

Mr Lambchop thought how exciting it would be to venture onto the same court with the champion. Signalling with his racket, he stepped forward.

'Okay.' Tom McRude handed over some balls. 'Let's see how you serve.'

Mr Lambchop prepared to serve.

'He's got his feet wrong!' Tom McRude shouted to the crowd. 'And his grip is wrong! Everything is wrong!'

This made Mr Lambchop so nervous that he served two balls into the net instead of over it.

'Terrible, terrible! Watch how I do it,' said Tom McRude, running to the far side of the court. From there, he served five balls in a row to Mr Lambchop, so hard and fast that Mr Lambchop missed the first four entirely. The fifth one knocked the racket out of his hand.

'Ha, ha!' laughed Tom McRude. 'Now let's see you run!'

He began hitting whizzing forehands and backhands at sharp angles across the court, making Mr Lambchop look very foolish indeed as he raced back and forth, getting redder and redder in the face and missing practically every shot.

The other Lambchops grew very angry as they watched, and Prince Haraz saw how they felt. 'This need not continue, you know,' he whispered to Stanley.

Just then, Mr Lambchop came skidding to a halt before them, banging his knee with his racket as he missed another of the champion's powerful shots.

'Ha, ha! This is how *I* give lessons!' shouted Tom McRude.

Mr Lambchop's eyes met Stanley's,
and then he looked at Prince Haraz.

'Okay,' Stanley said, and Prince Haraz
smiled his little smile again.

'Thank you,' said Mr Lambchop.

Returning to the court, he addressed the crowd. 'Ladies and gentlemen!' he said. 'I will try my serve again!'

Across the net, Tom McRude laughed a nasty laugh and slashed his big racket through the air.

Mr Lambchop served a ball, not into the net this time, but right where it was supposed to go, as fast as a bullet. Tom McRude could only blink as it went past him. Then his mouth fell open. 'Out!' he shouted. 'That ball was out!'

Voices rose from the crowd. 'Shame on you! . . . It was *in*! . . . What a liar! . . . In, in in!'

Tom McRude shook his fist at Mr Lambchop. 'I'll bet you can't do that again!'

Mr Lambchop served three more times, each serve even faster than the first one, and as perfectly placed. Tom McRude could not even touch them, except for the last, which bounced up into his nose.

Then Mr Lambchop began to rally with him, gliding swiftly about the court and returning every shot with ease. With powerful forehands and backhands, he made Tom McRude run from corner to corner; with little drop shots, he drew the champion up to the net, then lobbed marvellous high shots that sent him racing back again. Nobody has ever played such great tennis as Mr Lambchop played that day.

Tom McRude was soon too exhausted, and too angry, to continue. He threw down his racket and jumped on it, and hurled the broken pieces into the net.

'You're just lucky!' he yelled. 'Besides, I have a cold. And the sun was in my eyes the whole time!' He pushed his way through the crowd and ran out of the park.

There was tremendous clapping and cheering for Mr Lambchop, who just smiled modestly and waved his racket in a friendly way. Then he came over to where Stanley and Arthur and Mrs Lambchop and Prince Haraz were standing with the television director.

'You're really *good*,' the director said. 'Frankly, you looked terrible when you first went out there.'

'It takes me a while to get warmed up,' Mr Lambchop said, and led his family away.

In the excitement of the tennis, they

had all forgotten Mrs Lambchop's fame, but on the way home she was asked again and again for her autograph, and when they arrived, a photographer and reporter from *Famous Faces* magazine were waiting.

'We want you on the cover of our next issue,' said the photographer.

'I'm supposed to do an interview,' said the reporter. 'Who do you think is sexy? How much do you weigh? Eat health foods? Will there be a movie about your life? Who gave you your first kiss?'

'None of your business!' said Mr Lambchop, and Mrs Lambchop told the *Famous Faces* people to go away.

They all watched the evening news on television, hoping Mr Lambchop's amazing tennis would be shown, but

only Mrs Lambchop appeared, with Tom McRude in the background. 'The celebrated Harriet Lambchop was in the park today,' said the newscaster, after which there was a close-up of Mrs Lambchop saying, 'I hope all my fans are having a lovely day,' and that was that.

Mr Lambchop said he didn't care, but he did mind that dinner was interrupted several times by phone calls for Mrs Lambchop from newspaper and magazine and television people. The interruptions didn't bother the Liophant, who ate four pork chops, a jar of peanut butter, a quart of potato salad, and the rubber mat from under his dish.

## CHAPTER 4
## THE BROTHERS FLY

'I'm not complaining,' said Arthur, complaining, 'but it's not fair. Some people get to have Liophants and be famous. I want to be President, or as strong as Mighty Man, but all I got was one minute with an Askit Basket I'm not even allowed to use any more.'

He was talking to Stanley and Prince Haraz. It was after dinner, and they were in their bedroom, all in slippers and pyjamas.

'It's not my fault.' Prince Haraz looked hurt. 'A genie just follows orders. Rub, I appear. Wish, I grant. That's it.'

Stanley felt a little sorry for his brother. 'I don't think you ought to be President, Arthur,' he said. 'But I'll wish for you to be the strongest man in the world.' He nodded to Prince Haraz. 'Right now.'

'Oh, good!' Arthur said.

He waited, but nothing happened.

'Darn!' he said, 'I knew it wouldn't work!' Disappointed, he punched his left hand with his right fist.

'Owwww!' Jumping up and down, he waved his hand to relieve the pain.

'When you're the strongest man in the world,' Prince Haraz said, 'you have to be careful what you hit.'

'But I still feel like me,' Arthur said.

Testing himself, he took hold of the big desk with one hand and lifted. It rose easily into the air above his head.

Stanley's mouth flew open, and so did

the desk drawers. Pencils, paper clips, marbles, and other odds and ends rained down onto the floor.

'Oooops,' Arthur said, and lowered the desk.

'This is ridiculous,' said Prince Haraz, helping him to tidy up. 'The strongest man in the world, in his bedroom picking up desks! Out having adventures, that's where you ought to be.'

'We can't have adventures now,' Arthur said. 'It's almost bedtime.'

Stanley had an idea. 'There'd be time if we could fly! Why can't we all fly somewhere?'

'I've always been able,' said Prince Haraz. 'For you two, it'll take wishing.'

'I wish!' Stanley shouted. 'Flying! Arthur and me both!'

Full of excitement, the brothers held their breath, thinking they would be swept up into the air, but they weren't. After a moment, Arthur tried a few small flapping movements with his elbows.

'Oh, collibots!' said the genie. 'Not like that. Just *think* of flying, and where you want to go.'

It worked.

Stanley and Arthur found themselves
suddenly a few feet off the floor,
face down and quite comfortable,
and however they wished to go, up or
down, forward or back, was the way
then went. It was like swimming in soft,
invisible water, but without the effort of

swimming. After only a few minutes of practice, the brothers were gliding happily about the bedroom, with Prince Haraz giving advice: 'Point your toes, that helps . . . Heads up . . . Good, very good. Yes, I think you're ready now.'

He opened the window and leaned out. 'Nice enough,' he said. 'But there may be coolish winds higher up. We'd better wear something extra.'

Stanley and Arthur put on dressing-gowns and gloves, and the genie borrowed a red parka and a woollen dragon-face ski mask.

'Away we go!' he said, and the brothers floated through the window after him, out into the night.

Up! Up! Up! UP! they went, levelling off now and then to practise speeding,

but mostly rising steadily higher. Stanley
and Arthur flew side by side, gaining
confidence from each other, and the
genie kept an eye on them from behind.

It was a beautiful night. The sky above
them was full of stars, and the lights of
the city, far below, twinkled as brightly as
the stars. The brothers' white dressing-
gowns shone in the moonlight, and the
genie's parka was a glowing red.

They flew above the big park, where
an orchestra was giving a concert. Music
floated up to them: the clear, sweet tones
of flutes and violins and trumpets; the
deep, strong notes of cymbals and drums.

'Oh, I'm enjoying this!' Prince Haraz
called through his dragon mask. 'So
different from inside that lamp!'

They joined hands and circled together,

swooping and swaying in time to the music, going round and round above the blaze of light from where the orchestra sat. It was like ice-skating to music at a rink, but much more fun.

In the distance, the blinking wing lights of a big aeroplane moved steadily across the sky.

'Let's chase it!' Stanley shouted.

'Go on! I'll catch up!' Prince Haraz laughed and let them go.

*Whoooosh! Whoooosh!* With their arms by their sides, Stanley and Arthur flashed like rockets across the sky. Their dressing-gowns made little flapping sounds, like the sails of a boat racing before the wind.

The big aeroplane was fast, but the brothers were much faster. When they caught up, they were able to fly all around the plane, looking through the windows at the passengers reading and eating from tiny trays.

Arthur saw a little girl reading a comic magazine. Zooming in close to her window, he stretched his neck, trying to read over her shoulder. The little girl looked up and saw him. Being mean, she held the magazine down between her knees where he couldn't see it, and then she stuck out her tongue. Arthur stuck his tongue out at her, and the little girl scowled and pulled the curtain across her window.

On the other side of the plane, Stanley saw a young couple with a crying baby across their laps. They looked very tired, but they were being kept awake. Stanley flew up next to the window so that the baby could see him over its parents' shoulders, and then he made a funny face, puffing out his lips and wrinkling his nose. The baby smiled, and Stanley put his thumbs in his ears and wriggled his other fingers. The baby smiled again, and closed its eyes and went to sleep.

Stanley flew around the plane, past the cockpit, to join Arthur on the other side.

There were two pilots in the cockpit, and one of them saw Stanley fly by. Turning his head slowly, he saw both brothers hovering above a wing tip, waiting for Prince Haraz to catch up.

'Guess what I see out there, Bert,' he said.

'The stars in the sky, Max, and below us the mighty ocean,' answered the other pilot.

'No,' said Max. 'Two kids in dressing-gowns.'

'Ha, ha! You are some joker!' said Bert, but he turned to look.

Only Prince Haraz could be seen now above the wing, his parka flapping as he looked around for Stanley and Arthur, who were hiding from him behind the plane.

'So what do you see, Bert?' asked Max, keeping his own eyes straight ahead. 'Two kids in dressing-gowns, right?'

'Wrong,' said Bert quietly. 'I see a guy in ski clothes with a dragon face.'

The two pilots stared at each other, and then looked out at the wing again, but the genie had flown to join the boys behind the plane.

'Nobody there,' said Max. 'Let's never mention this to anyone, Bert. Okay?'

'Good idea,' Bert answered. 'Definitely.'

They made the plane go faster and had nothing more to say.

A giant ocean liner, ablaze with lights, made its way across the sea below.

'Come on!' Arthur shouted. He whizzed away, Stanley behind him, and again Prince Haraz laughed and let them go.

The size and beauty of the great ship made the brothers cry out in wonder as they drew near. It was like an enormous birthday cake, each deck a layer sparkling with the brightness of a thousand candles.

'Look, Stanley!' Arthur pointed. 'They're having a big party on the main deck!'

They flew closer to enjoy the fun, and then they saw that it was not a party, but a robbery.

The main deck was crowded because masked robbers had lined up all the passengers, and were taking their money and jewellery and watches. The helicopter in which the robbers had landed was parked just below the captain's bridge, which overlooked the main deck. The captain and the other ship's officers had been chained up on the bridge. They had struggled, but now there was nothing they could do.

'We've got to help, Stanley!' Arthur said.

He zoomed down to the bridge, and shouted over the railing at the robbers on the deck below. 'Stop, you crooks! Give back all that money and jewellery and other stuff!'

Using his great strength, Arthur tore away the ropes and chains that bound

the ship's officers. It was as easy for him
as if he were tearing up paper.

The robbers were amazed. Unable to
believe their eyes, they stumbled back
from their victims, dropping money and
jewellery all over the deck.

'Oh, lordy!' one robber yelled. 'Who
are you?'

Remembering his favourite comic-magazine hero, Arthur could not resist showing off. He flew ten feet up in the air and stayed there, looking fierce.

'I am Mighty Arthur!' he shouted in a deep voice. 'Mighty Arthur, Enemy of Crime!'

Exclamations rose from the robbers and passengers and ship's officers. 'So strong, and a flier too! . . . Who expected Mighty Arthur? . . . Are we ever lucky! . . . This ought to be on TV!'

Now Stanley came swooping down
from the sky with his dressing-gown belt
untied, so that the gown flared behind
him like a cape.

'And I'm Mighty Stanley!' he called.
'Defender of the Innocent!'

'I do that too!' cried Arthur, wishing
he had made his robe a cape. 'We
both do good things, but I'm the really
strong one!'

Several robbers were trying to escape
in the helicopter, and he saw another
chance to prove his strength.

The helicopter was already rising, but
Arthur flashed through the air until he was
directly above it, and with one hand he
pushed it back onto the deck. When the
frightened robbers jumped out, the ship's
officers grabbed them and tied them up.

Now the passengers were even more excited and amazed. 'Did you see that?' they said, and 'Mighty Arthur and Mighty Stanley, both on the same day!' and 'This is better than TV!'

The brothers flew up to join Prince Haraz, who had been circling over the ship. 'What a pair of show-offs!' said the genie, as they set out for home. 'Even worse than I used to be.'

Behind them, cheers floated up from the grateful passengers and crew. 'Hooray for our rescuers!' they heard, and 'Especially Mighty Arthur!' which was followed a moment later by 'Mighty Stanley too, of course!'

Soon the big ship was no more than an outline of tiny lights in the black sea below, and the last cheer was only a whisper above the rushing of the wind. 'Three cheers . . . for . . . the Enemy . . . of . . . Crime . . . and the . . . Defender . . . of the Inno . . . cent!'

The brothers felt very proud, but it had been a tiring adventure, and they were not sorry when the city came into sight.

## CHAPTER 5
## THE LAST WISH

When the three adventurers flew back into the bedroom, the Liophant was just finishing an enormous bowl of spaghetti mixed with chocolate cookies and milk. He looked sleepy, but Mr and Mrs Lambchop, standing by the door, were very much awake.

'Thank goodness you are all right!' Mrs Lambchop ran to hug her sons.

Mr Lambchop's voice was stern. 'Where

have you been? Is that you, Prince Haraz, behind that dragon face?'

The genie took off his ski mask. 'Were you worried?' he said. 'Sorry. We just went for a little flight.'

'Wait till you hear!' said Arthur. 'You can't tell from looking, but I'm the strongest man in the world, and −'

'First take off those dressing-gowns and gloves,' said Mrs Lambchop. 'It is not wise to get overheated.'

She went on talking while they put their things away. 'What a *dreadful* evening! The phone never stopped ringing. I was asked to go on six television shows, and to be in an advertisement for a new kind of soap − they wanted pictures of me in the bathtub, so of course I said no! − and to sit with the mayor during the next parade. I'm exhausted! And such a fright, after all that, to find the window open and the three of you gone!'

'We thought we'd be right back,' said Stanley, apologising. 'We didn't know so many exciting things would happen.'

Everyone sat down, and he explained about wishing Arthur strong, and the flying, not leaving out how they had chased the aeroplane and startled the robbers on the great ship at sea. Mr and Mrs Lambchop looked more and more worried as they listened, and when Stanley was done, Mr Lambchop gave a deep sigh.

'It seems, Prince Haraz,' he said, 'that there are often unexpected consequences when wishes come true.'

The genie nodded. 'I'll say. That's how I

got myself put into a lamp.'

'It is not just the difficulty about the Askit Basket,' Mr Lambchop said. 'Mrs Lambchop has been famous for only a day, and already it has exhausted her and cost our family its privacy. And though Tom McRude deserved the lessons he got, his tennis comes from natural ability, and I am not proud of having shamed him by the use of magic.'

'And now Arthur is so strong that other boys will be afraid to play with him,' said Mrs Lambchop. 'And this flying, and getting mixed up with criminals – Oh, it *is* worrying!'

'Indeed it is,' Mr Lambchop said. 'We must all think hard about what has happened, and what the future may bring.'

'I will make hot chocolate,' said Mrs Lambchop. 'It is extremely helpful when there is serious thinking to be done.'

Everyone enjoyed the delicious hot chocolate she brought from the kitchen,

with a marshmallow for each cup. Mr and Mrs Lambchop and Stanley and Arthur sat with their eyes half closed, sipping and thinking. Prince Haraz kept silent for a while, and then he said he was sorry to have caused problems, and began to pace up and down. The Liophant went to sleep.

At last Mr Lambchop put down his cup and cleared his throat. 'May I have your attention, please?' he said.

When they were all looking at him, he said, 'Here is my opinion. Genies and their magic, Prince Haraz, may be well suited to faraway lands and long-ago times, but the Lambchops have always been quite ordinary people, and this is the United States of America, and the time is today. We are grateful, I'm sure, for the excitement you have brought us, but I now believe that it would have been better for everyone if you had remained in your lamp. And so I must ask: Is it possible for Stanley to unwish the wishes he has made?'

'There is a way, actually,' said Prince Haraz, looking surprised.

Mrs Lambchop clapped her hands. 'How very wise you are, George! Don't you agree, boys?'

Arthur wasn't sure. 'I really like the flying,' he said, and then he sighed. 'But being so strong . . . I guess nobody *would* play with me.'

'What I care most about is the Liophant,' Stanley said. 'Couldn't we just keep him?'

'He *is* very lovable,' Mrs Lambchop said. 'But he *eats* so much! We cannot afford to keep him.'

'Sad, my dear, but true,' said Mr Lambchop. 'Now tell us, Prince Haraz, how we are to proceed.'

'It's called Reverse Wishing,' said the genie.

The little green lamp was still on the desk, and he picked it up and turned it over. 'The instructions should be right here,' he said. 'Let's see . . .'

The Lambchops waited anxiously as he studied the words that had been carved into the bottom of the lamp.

'Simple enough,' he said, after a moment. 'Each wish has to be reversed separately. I just say "Mandrono!" and −' His voice rose. 'Oh, collibots! Double florts! See that little circle there? This is a training lamp! There may not be enough wishes left!'

'What?' exclaimed Mr Lambchop. 'What's a training lamp?'

'They're used for beginners like me, so we don't do too much for one person,' Prince Haraz said unhappily. 'The number in the circle, the fifteen, that's all the wishes I'm allowed to grant Stanley.'

The Lambchops all spoke at once. 'What? . . . Only fifteen? . . . You never said! . . . Oh dear!'

'Please, I'm embarrassed enough,' said the genie, very red in the face. 'A training lamp! As if I were a baby!'

'We are all beginners at one time or another,' Mr Lambchop said. 'What matters now is, are fifteen wishes enough?'

Prince Haraz counted, folding his fingers to be sure he got it right. 'Askit Basket, Liophant – lucky he doesn't count double – that's two, and fame for Mrs Lambchop and the fancy tennis, that's four. Making Arthur strong, five, and flying for him *and* Stanley is two more . . .' He smiled. 'Seven, and seven for the reversing is fourteen! And we have a wish left over for some sort of goodbye treat!'

'Thank goodness!' said Mrs Lambchop.

'Could you manage all the reversing right now, please? It has grown very late.'

'I'll do the whole family in a bunch,' said the genie. 'Let's see. . . . Strength, famous, tennis, two flying. Ready, Arthur? No more Mighty Man after this, I'm afraid.'

'Will I feel weak?' Arthur asked. 'Will I

flop over?'

The genie shook his head. 'Mandrono!' he said. 'Mandrono, Mandrono, Mandrono, Mandrono!' Arthur felt a curious but not unpleasant prickling on the back of his neck. When the prickling stopped, he gave the big desk a shove, but it didn't move.

'I'm just the regular me again,' he said.

'Oh, well.'

'And I am just Harriet Lambchop again,' said Mrs Lambchop, smiling. 'An unimportant person.'

'To all of us, my dear, you are the most important person we know,' Mr Lambchop said. 'Arthur, you are as strong as you were yesterday. Think of it that way.'

Prince Haraz sipped the last of his hot chocolate. 'Where was I? Oh, yes . . .' He glanced at the Askit Basket, said, 'Mandrono!' and the basket was gone. 'That leaves just the Liophant,' he said.

The Lambchops all turned to look at the Liophant who was awake now and sitting up in the corner, trying to scratch behind his lion ears with the tip of his elephant trunk. Stanley went over and patted him, and the Liophant licked his hand.

'How sweet!' said Mrs Lambchop. 'George, perhaps . . .?'

'What makes Liophants happiest,' the genie said, 'is open spaces, and chasing unicorns, and wrestling with other Liophants.'

'Then send him where it's like that,' said Stanley, patting again. The Liophant vanished halfway through the pat.

For a moment no one spoke. Then Mr Lambchop put his hand on Stanley's shoulder in a sympathetic way. 'Good for you,' he said.

Stanley sat down to think about the one wish he had left, and Mrs Lambchop began to collect the hot chocolate cups. 'Where will you go, Prince Haraz, when you leave us?' she asked.

'Right back into that stuffy little lamp,' said the genie. 'And then it's just wait, wait, wait! Another thousand years, at least. It's a punishment I got for playing too many tricks. My friends warned me, but I wouldn't listen.'

Sighing, he handed Mrs Lambchop his

empty cup. 'Mosef, Ali, Ben Sifa, little Fawz. Such wonderful fellows! I think of them when I'm alone in the lamp, the fun they must be having, the games, the freedom . . .'

The genie's voice trembled, and he turned his head away. All the Lambchops felt very sorry for him.

Then Arthur had an idea. He ran across the room to whisper it to Stanley.

'Whispering?' said Mrs Lambchop. 'Where are your manners, dear?'

'Who cares?' Prince Haraz said crossly. 'Let's have that last wish, and I'll smoke back into my lamp.'

The brothers were smiling at each other.

'Good idea, right?' said Arthur.

'Oh, yes!' Stanley said.

He turned to the genie. 'Here is my last wish, Prince Haraz. I wish for you not to stay in the lamp, but to go back where you came from, so that you can be with your genie friends and have good times with them, forever from now on!'

Prince Haraz gasped. His mouth fell open.

Mr Lambchop worried that he might faint. 'Are you all right?' he asked. 'Is Stanley not allowed to set you free?'

'Oh, yes . . .' The genie's voice was very low. 'It's allowed. But whoever heard of . . . That is, nobody ever used up a wish for the sake of a genie. Not until now.'

'How very selfish people can be!' said Mrs Lambchop.

Prince Haraz rubbed his eyes. 'What a fine family this is!' he said, beginning to smile. 'I thank you all. The name of Lambchop will be honoured always, wherever genies meet.'

His smile enormous now, he shook hands with each of the Lambchops. The last shake was with Stanley, and the genie was already a bit smoky about the edges. By the time he let go of Stanley's hand, he was all smoke, a dark cloud that swirled briefly over the little lamp on the desk, and then poured in through the spout until not a puff remained.

Full of wonder, the Lambchops gathered about the lamp, and after a moment Arthur put his lips to the spout.

'Good-bye, Prince Haraz!' he called. 'Have a nice trip!'

From inside the lamp, faint and far away, a voice cried, 'Bless you, bless you all . . .' and then there was only silence in the room.

'I am proud of you, Stanley,' Mr Lambchop said. 'Your last wish was generous and kind.'

'It was my idea, actually,' Arthur said, and Mrs Lambchop kissed the top of his head.

Then she gathered the last of the hot chocolate cups and put them on her tray. 'Off to bed now,' she said. 'Tomorrow is another day.'

Stanley and Arthur got into bed, and she turned out the light.

'The lamp was supposed to be a surprise birthday present,' Stanley said sleepily. 'Now it won't be a surprise anymore.'

'I will love my present when you give it to me,' said Mrs Lambchop. 'And Prince Haraz was a tremendous surprise. Good night, boys.'

She kissed them both, and so did Mr Lambchop, and they went out.

The brothers lay quietly in the darkness for a while, and then Stanley sighed. 'I miss the Liophant a little,' he said. 'But I don't mind about the rest.'

'Me neither,' Arthur yawned. 'Florts, Stanley, and good night.'

'Good night,' Stanley said. 'Collibots.'

'Mandrono,' murmured Arthur, and soon they were both asleep.